Andrew's death

The pristine car pulled up at Walter's club adorned with high quality illumination to welcome its guests with pomp and splendor. Miss Angela Jones, a professional private detective, got out of her car casually and entered the club elegantly greeting everyone she saw coming up to her. The party was in full swing. Guests were busy gossiping amid light music, waiters were serving drinks and some dancers were giving their performance to orchestra. Angela was looking for some special person whose phone call had brought her here to see him. Soon, she caught the sight of a young boy waving to her.

He drew closer and greeted, "Hey! I'm Arian, Mr. Andrew's eldest son. I called you yesterday. I know you can help me find how my dad died. I'm not satisfied with the police investigation." His voice dropped. He looked at Angela's face fixedly, looking worried.

She said, "How do you know me?"

"You're a famous private detective. Everyone knows you. I'm sure you will help me." He replied.

She took a deep breath and continued to speak, "How many family members are you?"

"We were a happy family of four members. My mother, my father, my younger sister and I." answered Arian.

"What was he?"

"He was a jeweler. It's our family business."

"Where were you the night he was guest at Mathew's?"

"I was out of town for another business deal."

Arian looked more concerned to Angela than she had expected him to be. She thought he must have been closer to late Andrew Lawson.

"Miss Angela! Long time, no see!" Shouted the voice behind her back.

To her surprise, it was her college class fellow, Brian. She beamed at him, appreciating his intimacy.

"It's so pleasing to see you here at the party, Brian!" Angela exclaimed cheerfully.

"I come here more often, but I've never seen you here before. By the by, I'm glad to see you after a long time."

"I came to Warkington last week, Brian. I usually do not attend busy parties, you know, I have only just come to see Walter's club vibes. It is a Saturday night and I love watching the Saturday night of this club."

Brian looked long at Angela as if he had been trying saying something he could not have externalized. She wanted to keep him company, but she had to make her way home.

She made her exit through the hustle bustle of the club hastily, keyed her car and drove off. Angela's cell phone rang while she was driving and thinking of her client. She took the call which, she was sure of, was Arian's.

"I want to see you somewhere tomorrow." He voiced on her cell.

"Come to Mundala restaurant at 1 pm.tomorrow." Angela spoke into her cell to him.

She gathered speed, turning on some music, making sure that she would get home on time to spend the weekend with her mum who had been waiting for her to return home. While driving, she was distracted into her new case that was although not a challenge. Her car sped up on the main roads leading her to her residence, Fulmer Villa, house no.54, West Lawrence Street. She pulled up at her garage and headed in with some gift for her beloved mother.

"Hi mum! See I've brought you a new wrist watch you have wished to get." Angela enthused.

Her mother was a handicapped woman of 60 and she had lost her husband in her youth. Mrs. Anne Jones brought up Angela singlehandedly to become a cop like her husband. Angela always wished to go into a private intelligence agency, as she was more inclined towards adventure and detection.

Her mother looked smilingly at Angela, "You are a better gift for me than this watch. Thanks! My love! By the way, how was your day?" Mrs. Jones remarked and inquired.

"Nothing special, a kind of busy day as usual." Her voice trailed off as if she wanted to close her conversation.

Mrs. Anne ordered the maid to lay the table for dinner. After dinner, Angela rolled into her room and played the recording on her cell to listen to the information on Mr. Andrew's last meeting with Mr. Mathew that her assistant, Rebecca, had shared with her following Arian's phone call. The information was a statement of Mr. Mathew's servant who waited on them at tea party.

The recording sounded, "He was ere talking to boss over tea about some jewel. He was wurrid he had no time.......that's all I oveherd."

It was a substantial evidence that Mr. Andrew had some problem that had been gnawing away at his confidence. She made a call to Rebecca to glean information on his family and friends. After a prolonged reflection, she drifted off to sleep in bed.

The next morning brought her a new investigation spree. Although it was Sunday, it would not allow her a full family time. Soon after a hearty breakfast, she got out to reach her office at Star Square. She swept out of her car gracefully, her cell phone swinging in her soft-skinned hands. The building was not much crowded with people, as it was a day off. She entered the elevator, hit the fifth floor button and rode it to her office.

The door opened and she was greeted, "Good day! I've found out that Mr. Andrew Lawson was a family man and his family members loved him dearly. Mrs. Andrew...I mean Monica was his second wife and she bore him a daughter, Moira. Arian and Moira are stepsiblings. Mr. Mathew Peter is also a well off jewel trader, who was always Mr. Andrew's best friend. One strange fact of his personality is that Mr. Andrew Lawson was a necromancer." Rebecca filled her in.

"It means he knew that he might run into a danger." Angela muttered to Rebecca.

"Yes, may be…"

"Let's go to his home. Get our paraphernalia!"

Revelations

Angela was on her way to Mandala restaurant where she was supposed to be at 1 pm. Rebecca was to remain in car to record Arian's conversation with Angela who had bluetooth on her person. Her car was whizzing past the traffic when, all of a sudden, a speeding bike swerved across and the rider signaled her to pull over. She braked her car on the light traffic road at his gesture. He pulled a gun at her, asking her to get out of the car. She swiftly emerged as directed and looked at him. He accosted her and put his gun to her temple.

He whispered, "Make with your cell phone, baby!"

Rebecca was still seated in the front composed and relaxed. She was sure of her mistress. Angela was best at Kungfu and Martial arts, she was only twenty five, but she was not short on brains.

Angela twisted his arm in the blink of an eye and yanked at the pistol. He leapt at her with all his strength, failing to strike her. Angela performed a backflip, deflecting his blows. She charged at his posture and punched his lights out. He crashed to the ground hard-blown. Rebecca got out to pick up the pistol with a handkerchief. They resumed their seats and drove off to Mandala.

In the restaurant, Arian was waiting for her. She reached his table and was greeted with a smile. Arian had something to tell her about his late father. He narrated, "My dad loved me. He had no rivals in business. Even, he was a necromancer. How was he poisoned and killed?" Arian broke down in tears.

"I think you have something to tell me. Please come to the point!"

"A week before his death he told me that he was cheated. I was shocked. He was disheartened and disconcerted. He told me that his friend, Mr. Mathew, had shattered his trust and his wife, I mean, my step mom, had been cheating on him for years." Arian stopped short.

"How do I believe you? Any proof!" She demanded.

"Yes, my step sister was also there. You can check with her." Arian assured her.

"How had he not found it out much earlier? By your own account, he could talk to the spirits." Angela argued.

"He learnt necromancy from someone after his car accident, four years back." Arian added.

"Alright!" Angela breathed deeply.

"Thank you for your time! I think this information will help you move on."

She proceeded to her car outside the restaurant and joined Rebecca. They drove to Lawson House thereafter.

On the way, Angela wondered who that rider was, why Arian did not share this latest information of Mr. Andrew's secret of his friend and his wife at Walter's club last night. She thought that perhaps it might have been too embarrassing for him to speak of that secret at the club. Probably, Arian wanted some time to share it. Different ideas flooded her mind en route to Andrew Lawson's residence. Half an hour later, Angela and Rebecca got to his abode. They met Mrs Monica Andrew who was a fashionable lady of 40 and very soft spoken.

"How can I help you?" Monica eyed them, inquiring about their visit to her.

"This is Angela Jones! I'm a detective from Anti-crime agency. I want to know the reason for late Andrew's death. Was he sick? Was he suicidal?"

"Nothing of the sort he was. He was a lovely family man. He had a heart arrest." Monica satisfied Angela's curiosity.

"How long have you been married?" Angela asked as if she were an anchor person.

"We have been married for 18 years. We loved each other. We were a happy family. His death has already been investigated and the police have closed the case. It was a heart failure. He was a cheery fellow. He had no business problems either." Monica retorted.

"Thank you for your cooperation and time." She expressed.

Rebecca looked around Mr. Andrew's bungalow, thinking of any possible clue that might have escaped the closed police probe. Angela did not seem eager about any more enquiries. She was only interested in late Mr. Andrew's recent phone calls.

Story of 'Pyrus'

The next morning Angela and Rebecca were attempting to unravel the cause of Mr. Andrew's death in their office when they learned all of his outgoing and incoming phone calls. The special number he frequently contacted was that of a famous necromancer's, Devin Yukol's, whose details were rather obscure to access within a short while.

"Mr. Devin Yukol, a renowned sorcerer who is now far away. What was he to Mr. Andrew? Why was he contacted?" whispered Rebecca to Angela.

"We'll get to know the answers to your questions on listening to the call recordings. Don't worry! Rebbie! I've been granted the permission to get them." She assured Rebecca. They were sitting at the office table, perusing their deceased client's file for every significant detail. The hot coffee was served to them to solve their case at their ease. A few minutes later, the office door flung open and Brian entered with a broad smile on his face. He looked exquisitely handsome in his black office suit and shining loafers, swinging his broad arms as if to ask them about their progress in this latest case. "What has become of Mrs. Monica? Was Arian right about her infidelity?" Brian shot up his eyebrows, questioning Angela.

She looked up at him and answered, "It was just an allegation. He wishes to prove her guilty about infidelity or something, so he is clear of any suspicions. I knew it, Brian, the moment he called me first time. The way he was talking about his father's death was very strange. I mean he was sure his father, Mr. Andrew Lawson, was murdered and he wasn't satisfied with the formal investigation. Arian has wanted me to go his way, catch Mrs. Monica and Mr. Mathew Peter. Now there is a new character, Mr. Devin Yukol. Thanks for your appearance at the Walter's party as my long lost college fellow. It was a good idea of distracting stalkers."

 "You are welcome! I have some information to share with you now." Brian added.

"Please go ahead!" Angela prompted him.

"Mr. Arian is badly involved with this person, Mr. Devin Yukol. Mrs. Andrew is not in the picture, even her young daughter, Moira, is out of picture. You have also found out she is mentally retarded. Mr. Mathew is a well-to-do jewel trader and your investigation proves he has had nothing to do with the deceased friend of his. Angie! You devolved to me the task of Mr. Andrew's will. For your information, he has bequeathed all his property to his wife, Mrs. Monica Andrew Lawson. You will be surprised to know Arian is sure you can learn the hang of this case very quickly. It was Arian's mugger to get the measure of you on your way to Mandala restaurant." Brian paused.

"What does Arian think about my dealing with the case?"

"He's rather scared you will find the truth. He thinks he has made a mistake of hiring you to probe his father's death or may be murder. On approaching you first he never had the idea you would take things your own way. Later, he realized you might fathom out the truth."

"Do you have any idea of Davin Yukol's origins?" Angela added another question.

"Yes! He is the one who taught Mr. Andrew the skill of talking to the dead. He is from Rumaan. Arian has been asking him to help him get all of his father's property for eight years. It was Arian's plan to have him killed in the car accident four years ago, but his plan went awry and Mr. Andrew survived. After this accident he became skeptical and superstitious. He insisted that he should learn to talk to his dead wife and Arian introduced him to Mr. Yukol."

Angela looked at her assistant with a puzzled expression. Rebecca sipped her coffee as Brian closed his conversation. The office door shot open again and another cup of hot coffee was brought in. It was for Brian. He always loved having a cup of hot coffee while talking out any case with his colleagues. Angela offered him his favourite coffee, but he refused with repugnance. Angela's surprise mounted too exceedingly to keep it back from Brian.

"Why don't you have coffee with us, Brian?" She addressed him insistently.

"I don't want to, Angie!" He responded.

Brian backed off and stood aside from their office table. All of his actions looked very strange to his colleagues who had never seen him so uncomfortable with coffee. Both ladies noticed that Brian was unwell. He drew himself further away and made his exit, leaving them guessing.

Angela followed him, sensing some danger and calling out to Brian. She took the elevator that appeared just there, flinging herself uncontrollably into it to hit the ground floor button.

It was not long before she got to the basement of Star Square packed with cars and noticed that there was some silhouette behind the pillar. She paced up to spot the eerie glow that emanated from the silhouette transitioning into a half human-beast figure on fire.

"What is this?" She gave a shrill cry.

"Pyrus! Disguised as your Brian." A strident voice carried to her from this creature.

"What're you talking about? Where is Brian Richard?"

"Possessed and then killed by me!" The fiery-beastly creature snarled at Angela.

The weird fiery creature moved on to her, clad in a black cloak covering his gigantic form that was becoming visible to her. His red shot bulging eyes were set on a large protruding countenance. He went on, "Close your investigation now!"

On the spur of the moment, her hand reached her gun on her person which she aimed at him. Pyrus looked nerveless and still. Angela pumped six bullets into him, but to no avail. He disappeared, but the gunshots brought everyone down panicked and perplexed. She rushed off to her car, thinking about Brian and leaving all her office staff behind. The car drove away to Regent Street, Mr. Andrew's bungalow, to see Arian who she believed was responsible for it. She had tears in her eyes recalling her bonding with Brian, her trust in him and their days of training together. Her car was parked at the main gate to Lawson House. She got out of her car in a huff and gained entry into his residence. She was received by Mrs. Monica who wanted to know why Angela was there all of a sudden. Angela asked her grimly where Arian was in the house. Monica pointed at his room upstairs and Angela raced up. She stormed into his room and found him waiting for her.

"What have you done to Brian? Who is Pyrus?"

"Take it easy, madam! Your lover is dead. Pyrus is my slave. I mean our slave….Davin Yukol's slave. Davin and I are best friends. That's why I said, 'our slave'. You know everything Pyrus has told you as Brian is right. You beat up my mugger, my man and I was sure you were going to catch me. I talked to my friend. He helped me to get the better of you. One by one everyone close to you will be killed at the hands of Pyrus, our slave, till you stop your hand on this case. Choice is yours." Arian heaved a sigh of relief, looking over her with vanity in his eyes.

Angela contained herself, demanding the proof of Brian's death, "Show me the proof of his death."

"Interesting! Check out your hand phone just now. You'll get to know." Arian snapped rather indifferently.

She had nothing to do with any more enquiries except retreat into her business. Heading back to her office, she called Rebecca to say that Brian was dead. In the meanwhile, Star Square Anti-crime had discovered a burnt and ripped dead body which was Brian's. Rebecca and her department had identified it before Angela's phone call, but she was so aggrieved and agitated that she could not open up on Brian's murder. Landing on fifth floor was as hard for Angela as setting foot on a mountain, dejected and disconcerted Angela Jones stretched her legs to her office and sat at her table. In no time, she brought out her hand phone, played the video shared by Arian with disbelief and horror in her eyes, not waiting for her other colleagues to join in with her. He was struck, burnt and mutilated in the video. To her astonishment, there was no one attacking him whenever he received a blow, another blow and laceration. She could see that he was ablaze from nowhere and his cries and screams went unheard. The video was incredibly painful to watch. She now thought back of her last conversation with that gruesome imposter that flinched away from the hot coffee.

"Why was he repelled?" She looked straight at the cup of coffee for him, thinking deeply to herself.

Just then, the whole staff filed into her office, looking challenged and despondent, accompanied by Mr. Hudson Royal who was the chief investigation officer.

"Angela! We've brought Mr. Mathew Peter with us. He has something strange to tell us." Mr. Hudson revealed to her.

Mathew Peter came forth and greeted them with melancholy in his voice. All investigation team huddled around him, preparing to listen to his information. Angela and Mr. Hudson came in front of him and asked him to sit. He sat down comfortably and was requested to begin his talk. The team started to record.

He cleared his throat and spoke, "Andrew and I were labours in Rumaan many years ago. We worked for a rich man who always paid us high wages. We both were good friends too. One day a stranger came into our village and he told our master to dig up the ruined castle in his village. Our master sent both of us to his place to work for him. Andrew and I dug up his castle for three days without knowing what to extract from the castle grounds. The fourth day we found gold and jewels deep in the grounds. We were overjoyed. We decided to steal the treasure and run away soon, but we thought about our families in our hometown. We changed our minds and told the stranger, called Taylon, of what we had found. He became happy with us and gave us lots of gold and jewels. He was the owner of the ruined castle which was haunted by many Jinns. No one wanted to work for him, so he got to our master. We returned to our town rich and happy. Our lives changed. We took leave of our master and moved here. We settled as jewel traders here. Behind our back, Taylon gave a large share of the treasure to our master. But he was killed by those Jinns who haunted the old castle. One of the most powerful of them was called Pyrus. He was said to have come from an emerald which had been lying deep in the castle grounds. We never knew how that Jinn had emerged and who had got that special emerald. Yes, luckily, Andrew was said to hold the other emerald which was believed to be the end of Pyrus. Last time, he saw me and he was very depressed about the possession of that emerald. He said he was uneasy as if under some spell."

"Where's that emerald now?" Asked Angela curiously.

"It was in the custody of his late wife. She had kept it safe somewhere. Fella Andrew found that emerald different. I mean she'd say that the gem had 'Pyrus' engraved on it. Unfortunately, she died soon after we'd come here." Mathew replied.

"Did she leave it with Andrew for safekeeping?" Mr. Hudson took his turn in interrogation.

"I think not. Andrew actually didn't know where the gem really was and this is why he wanted to communicate with his wife after her death. He learned necromancy from someone and…" Mathew stopped short, rasping.

Mathew's statement solved the mystery of Pyrus and Andrew's logic of learning necromancy. The team also concluded that Davin Yukol must be the one that had got the hold of the first emerald. It was now clear to Anti-crime agency that Devin Yukol wished to control and rule the whole world, having to get Pyrus immortal at his disposal and Arian wanted to inherit all his father's property, putting his step mother and his late father's business partner into trouble forever.

Mathew Peter was relieved of the further investigation and was sworn to secrecy. Angela, Mr. Hudson and Rebecca were in full action and they decided to talk to Arian now.

"I'm sure he'll want us to charge Monica and Mathew with Andrew's murder." Rebecca remarked.

"Let me call him according to our plan." Angela burst out resolute.

The phone call was made to Arian. He picked up the call and purred, "Thank you for calling me! I know you want to close the case. Great! Miss Angela, you're now going to accuse the real culprits. So sweet! You've seen the horror of Brian's accidental death.

Come here and hand me the investigation outcome as soon as possible."

He closed his talk and the call ended, exactly the way they had anticipated.

"Before we move on, we must get the other gemstone." Mr. Hudson whispered.

"You're right, sir! How can we gain access to that emerald? His wife who kept it is dead. Andrew even wanted to know of it." Rebecca wondered.

"The most important step is to agree to Arian's terms to avoid any more killing. Monica and Mathew can be put under investigation just to his pleasing."

Mathew was on his way home, calling up his friendship and partnership with his dead friend when the sudden thought of visiting their office occurred to him. He directed his driver to drive up to Andrew-Mathew Jewelers. In no time, he was in the office which was their meeting room. He sat down at the table, staring at it and leafing through Andrew's log book. One of the pages caught his attention to the note by Andrew. It read, "I communed with Fella about the emerald which was on her right hand index finger in her coffin. She was buried with it." He tore it out of the log book and decided to turn it in to Anti-crime agency.

Mathew hastened to Star Square with the latest information for the investigation team. He strode across the foyer into Mr. Hudson's office where the discussion was still ongoing. He seemed to have run out of patience and burst, "I've got to know where the other gem is." His sentence resounded and captivated everyone's attention.

"Where's it?" Asked Mr. Hudson.

"In Fella's coffin, on her index finger." Mathew answered, producing the paper from his pocket. "You can see for yourself." He added sounding a little comfortable.

The log book page was studied meticulously. The hand writing on the page was checked with Andrew's hand writing, the date on the page was February, 23 which was the day before his death and the texture of the note was also considered as a quick word to share. It changed hands for further reviews until it was deemed genuine.

At last, one of the officers, Mr. Gerald Dow nodded. Angela looked at Mathew and began to speak, "He's been dead for ten days now, but you've found it just today. I wonder how it's happened."

"I haven't been attending office since Andrew's death. I've been dealing with business at home instead. I didn't even see him on 23rd, so I had no information of it." He explained.

They discussed their plan with Mathew and he gave his consent. The next step was to declare Mrs. Monica Andrew guilty of her husband's murder. She was to be taken into confidence. The last step was to get that emerald ring from Fella's grave, destroy it, arrest Davin Yukol for Brian's murder, Andrew's murder and arrest Arian. But it was not an easy plan to execute. Extreme and intensive care was required to carry it out.

The police were informed of their investigation report and Mathew and Monica were apprehended. Now, Angela and Rebecca were entrusted with the surreptitious disinterment the following night.

Devin Yukol in the cemetery

The following night Angela and Rebecca arrived in the municipal cemetery on the hill. The large area was taken up by the run down cemetery full of tumbled gravestones. Both visitors followed by two masons inched forward picking their way carefully, shining their torches on each and every gravestone that bore the letters, "Fe...". After half an hour's walk the gravestone of "Fella Andrew" was sighted. The grave was old and dusty and built no farther away from a secluded church. Angela ordered the two men to disinter Fella's grave as it started to rain. Rebecca and Angela looked intently at the men at work while the lightning flashed in the sky and a weird-looking man with a hat on showed up on slab at the side of the grave. He came forward and called out, "I'm Devin Yukol! Thank you for helping me find my jewel. What can I do for you?"

"How're you here?" Rebecca interrogated.

"I have been asked by Narcis, my jinni, who has been spying on Mathew, to come here and get my treasure." The man replied, looking around and pointing at a hideous creature behind him. He doffed his hat and chanted some incantation, transforming his slave creature into Angela's mother, Anne Jones. It made Angela shout at him, "You can't do any harm to my mother!"

The sights and sounds of terror had already repelled the two men. Both women were at the mercy of the weather and witchcraft. Rebecca pulled out her gun of her coat and aimed at the man. He seemed unafraid with Narcis at his service. He looked at them sternly and said, "Go away from here! I could have got my jewel earlier than you came. I want to warn you off coming in my way. I know that you wish to destroy my Pyrus. You wish to blow my cover and ruin me. Remember I will ravage you if you even wish to ruin me. Finally, I have something to show you." He looked at his jinni. The creature changed into her former self. Her grotesque, dark round countenance lit up. It was glowing, revealing Angela's mother crying in agony. The scene of horror swept over her and she begged, "Please let go of her!" Her courage and confidence had ebbed away. She only thought of her mother.

Devin laughed raucously, "Strange! You want to get that gem to kill Pyrus and there he wishes to kill your mother brutally. Go and save her. She is calling you." Rebecca put her right hand onto Angela's head in an attempt to console her, holding gun in her left hand. She muttered, "I'd rather you saved your mother. I'm going to get the emerald ring from Fella's grave."

"It's not possible! I can't leave you alone in danger here."

"Don't be silly! I'll hold him back. His monster will kill your mom if stay here, go, get home fast."

"Right! I am going to go, but our office driver can help you. He's in the car out there. I'm sending him to you. I'll be back pronto."

Rebecca stood still pointing her gun at Devin. He did not bother having to respond to their private conversation, or being a target. All he thought about was to get the emerald from the coffin in the grave. Rebecca watched Angela drawing back carefully. The rain was still falling with strong winds. The only detective stared at her rivals; the sorcerer and his demoness. She shouted, "I can't let you have it." Her gun fired but in vain. Devin was levitating the coffin regardless of gunshots that were being pumped into his body. He was intact and focused on his task while she leapt at the dead body's coffin, trying reaching all over it to struggle with Devin's levitation. The sight of an inferior struggler, reaching out to his gem invited the covetous wizard's rage. Devin Yukol snarled, "Rip her out! Narcis! Enough is enough!" The jinni in attendance on him threw herself at the coffin in the form of a large chameleon and settled on poor Rebecca's sprawled body clinging to the coffin-edges, tearing out her tissues. Enfeebled and wounded, Rebecca cried out for help before Devin whose powers witched out the emerald ring of the corpse's finger to him. The feeling of superiority and victory shot through him as a hard stone hit his hand. The emerald ring catapulted high in the air and landed into the secluded church. The action was so abrupt and sudden that the wizard could not detect the source of that stone. Within a split second, Devin rose as high as the ring, but he failed to clutch at it and bumped into the old church wall that pitched him off. Devin Yukol was stunned at all this momentum. In the meanwhile, an agile and young man appeared in sight, coming to Rebecca's rescue. The demoness let go of her and lunged forward to attack the young man who was puffing at his cigarette and swaggering up defiantly.

Devin Yukol regained his balance and sense to confront this intruder and saviour. It was the first time that someone had bearded the lion in his den. The sight of her car driver, Faizan, relieved Rebecca and breathed a new life into her. She managed to scramble down the coffin to the gravestone to rest when Narcis approached Faizan but she retreated suddenly. Her master looked at the church and left the scene to get the hold of his precious emerald that meant his immortality. Devin flew over to the church casement, yet he could not gain access. Devin changed his mind, blowing some mantra under his breath around the abandoned church. The bold young man had tossed his cigarette at the monster to fend for himself. Devin and Narcis disappeared suddenly as if they had given up on their mission.

Pyrus kills Anne Jones

Angela rushed home panting and gasping. The main gate to Fulmer Villa was open, which indicated to her that someone had entered her home. Without further ado, she ran into her house and found her housemaid lying bleeding on the lounge floor. She felt her pulse flipping her body supine. Her maid was dead now. She dashed towards her mother's room which was illuminated and resounded with loud conversation. The sight of her happy mother confused her mind. She had been assuming the worst all her way home. She backed off, making no noise and hid behind the refrigerator.

"What is this? Who is mum talking to?" Angela asked herself, looking spellbound.

She stayed hidden, popping out her head to get the view of the other person her mother was talking to. That was Angela herself. The sight of herself close to her mother made her shudder; her throat parched, her eyes wide open in disbelief and body completely pale and numb. She froze in terror.

"It must be Pyrus, the imposter, the beast that killed Brian." She thought to herself. By the time her mind was still concluding, she was touched gently. In horror, she turned round and screamed with fright at Devin Yukol just close to her.

"This horror and this terror please me too much. Your confusion, your perplexity and your disconcertment help my slaves with their feeding frenzy. Your mother is dead." Devin raged furiously.

"You can't do this to me! My mom is all the world to me. Say this is false." She choked with high emotions and broke down in tears, sinking down to her knees.

Her happy mother swiftly shape shifted into Narcis and her own self shape shifted into Pyrus. The sorcerer ordered her dead mother's body by clapping. Angela had scarcely mustered her strength when Arian came into sight with Anne Jones's body in his arms. Her mother was brutally mutilated.

She shuffled languishingly to her mother whose words and actions had filled her life with innumerable joys. She reached out to her dead body and gathered her into her arms. Angela began to cry like a small child before her spectators.

"What a play by Miss Angela? What a performance?" Arian clapped amid the tragedy. He continued, "I was a fool, boss, I trusted her. Had you not told me of her plan, I would have been an object of ridicule."

"I was wrong. I hadn't reckoned on your powers. The plan was destructive, but the investigation report was in your favour." She sobbed and gave a pause.

Her vacant eyes rested on Arian's face and she puffed on, "Andrew had left the will for Monica, arresting her for your father's murder was a folly. We remarked in the report your father had died intestate, the will was a forgery on her part. All business and property was yours. "

"Nevertheless you carried out my wish, you were against me. It was short-lived. You were going to trap me soon." Arian rapped at her.

The wizard seemed indifferent to this conversation and stormed out followed by Arian, leaving a grieving daughter defeated and devastated.

She looked at her mother's lifeless face, kissed her forehead and swore to avenge her murder. She was unable to move a limb with her dead mother in her arms. Angela leaned against the wall, traumatized by the episode. Meanwhile, the police and news channels had surrounded Fulmer Villa, her residence.

The news that Miss Angela Jones's mother and housemaid were murdered by alleged Jason's gang in her absence had spread like wild fire. Amid the din of police vans and hospital ambulance her office driver arrived only to see Angela and talk to her. Anti-crime agency team officers pleaded with high officials there to allow them to talk to her, as it was urgent.

In the house, the paramedic staff had picked up both the corpses and stretchered them off. Angela was carried into her room and seated in a recliner by the side table. She realized that she had responsibilities for her life and parent. Suddenly, her eyes met the wrist watch which was gifted to her dearest mother the other day. Her eyes wandered over the watch as she extended her hands to it. The watch reminded her of that lovely evening she had brought it for her mother. Angela felt and fondled her mother's watch until she noticed the emblem of 'Gems of Rumaan' under the dial.

Her close look at her mother's watch determined that there were precious gems in the dial of the watch. She stood up, closed the door under the pretense of going to sleep and returned to examine it. Her words of idle mind issued from her lips while scrubbing the dial and looking at it. All of a sudden, her room was filled with some uncanny pall of fog forming in a light figure of indeterminate configuration. As soon as the pall cleared, Angela was able to see a humongous cloudy bear-like figure that she believed to have appeared from this watch.

"Whatever it is. It must serve me now." She mumbled, glaring at the cloudy energy as if wanting to master it. No sooner had she moved her gaze than the magnificent energy entered her body and mind. She felt herself levitating a little. Angela lit on the idea of putting this watch on her right hand. She wore it, absorbing all the energies from it under the sway of its gems. Her mind began to command her faculties most strongly.

Her vision began to move furniture in her room. She resolved to keep it secret.

Out of Fulmer Villa Angela's colleagues were still seeking the permission from the police officers for their entry which was eventually granted. Mr. Hudson Royal and Faizan Akhter were allowed to talk to her. Their ingress into her room was a relief to Angela. Her chief offered his condolences to her avuncularly, but she wanted to know of Rebecca and the finger ring. The office driver,

Faizan Akhter, told her about the gem having blown into the cemetery church. He said that Devin could not get it and that emerald was still in the church. He also told Angela about Rebecca's death. They stopped as Angela burst into sobs and tears. Mr. Hudson and the latter were too overrun to say anymore. They left her and made their way, hoping for Angela to come to terms with this grave consternation.

Angela got out of her room and expressed her wish to join in with her team to carry out her duty with earnest humbleness.

Renewed Angela

After the funeral of her mother in her town cemetery where her father had long been buried she resigned herself into a local park to ruminate over the events in her life. Her only objective was now to get the better of Devin and Arian. Angela wanted to punish them the way they had persecuted her colleagues, housemaid and dearest mother. She was treading in the park with her head full of her analysis of all the situations that had been occurring in the course of the recent killings. She could think how Pyrus dreaded the hot coffee, how her fear of the shape shifters defeated her, how Faizan's stone throw baffled Devin. It was becoming easy to understand now. Satisfied with her conclusion, she seated herself on a park bench lonely and lost just then an eerie glow began to appear before her. She seemed to flinch and fear first, but she soon gathered that it was her new companion from her magic watch she had on her wrist.

The glow was taking a form of a subtle hallow heightening as it approached her imperceptibly. Angela remained composed so as not to attract attention, waiting for its full development. The glowing hallow moved closest to her. It blew something on her face and vanished. Her mind could interpret its message as the 'confrontation with her opponents'. She was clear what she would do next.

Immediately afterwards, Faizan called on her to drive her to Star Square. She was morose in the car while he was elaborating on the event in the cemetery. He was willing to retrieve the emerald ring only if she approved. Angela did not seem to respond to his idea. She was not disposed to go on any topic in the car, feeling uncertain about any course of action. The driver made a stop, pulling up into the parking space. She stepped up into her office and was greeted warmly.

"Good day! We have something to discuss with you." Greeted Mr. Hudson and staff.

She looked grim opening up, "I don't want to participate in any discussion which is void. I am afraid, sir, you never know that every thing is conveyed to Arian and his accomplice."

"Do you want to give in to them?" Mr. Gerald questioned her, scratching his brow.

"I am going to combat you right there! I know you...Narcis. You are here! I can feel you eavesdropping on us here. I will get back at Devin, Arian and you" Angela shouted out walking around her office, looking to and fro for her addressee.

"What is this nonsense? How can you say this? You are an officer." Mr. Gerald sounded annoyed, staring at her.

He went on, "If take law into your hands, we'll have to relieve you of your services and you know...." He paused as if feeling unjust.

"Sir, I will never overstep the line. It is the message to Devin's messenger that is a jinn. All our previous underhand plans have been conveyed by his invisible creatures that work for him. I just beg you to leave this case with me only. I can deal with it." Angela sounded anxious.

Mr. Hudson and Mr. Gerald consulted each other on her plea. They also talked to other officers. In the meanwhile, Angela got out of her office, not wanting to interpose herself among them. A moment later, Mr. Hudson opened the office door and invited her in.

She was vested in all her authority. Mr. Hudson was confident that she would tackle this challenge viably. He came up to her and patted her on her back, "You can do it. We all are proud of you. You have always been winning. You have always been solving difficult cases before. But, you know, this case involves supernatural intervention and we need to be extra careful. Rebecca is no more. So we wish to associate Faizan Akhter with you. He thwarted the devilish grasp and braved the forces."

"Your wish is my command, sir!" She conceded.

Confrontation

Devin Yukol was wise to her forthcoming action. He did not will to visit the cemetery until Angela made her next entry although he had been longing to get his gem as soon as possible. He had challenged her to call on the cemetery church the evening her mother was laid in peace. It was Devin's message that she had received by her hermit. Angela was fully prepared to meet her foes that evening.

She arrived in the cemetery. Her mind and body combined together to provide the strength for her mission. She was crossing over, leaping on and plodding through the tumbledown graves that came in her way. Hastening her legs to near the abandoned church, she finally spotted her host.

"Welcome, my dearest and nearest Miss Angela Jones! How do you think you can stop me getting my treasure and achieving my aim?" Devin growled daringly.

The appearance of Arian drawing off the church and closing up to Devin confirmed her reservation that her opponent did not want to miss the opportunity of outwitting her. She could see the emerald ring in his right hand.

"Hi! Do you like this surprise?" Arian jeered at her, flaunting the ring.

He handed it to his boss who picked it reverently and put it on his index finger.

"I am eternal and immortal now!" Devin's voice echoed through the town. He looked victoriously at her, overstretching his arms and summoning his behemoth to his service. He ordered, "Come here, my Pyrus, you are immortal now!"

The horizon brightened up with a dark cloud hovering above Angela. The lightening flashed across the sky.

The dark cloud descended, metamorphosing into hideous, enormous, shapeless demon. She felt the hateful creature's presence behind her.

She smiled and congratulated Devin Yukol, "I am not here to take my revenge on you. I am here to join you because I am also a witch now."

Devin came closer to her, withdrawing his slaves from command. He was completely bewildered, scanning her face.

He gave a loud laugh ridiculing her and said, "Oh! Really! Do you think I am a fool?"

"I was a fool, wasting my life idly making enemies of me. Just believe me I have changed a lot. I wish to marry you and live happily with you." She said confidently.

"Great mind! Great idea! But what about the words you said to our Narcis in your office? 'I'm coming to get back at you..' What a design?" Arian clapped, looking at his boss.

"Did she say these words to our slave, boss?"

"I am really impressed. It means my messenger was mistaken. You love me." Devin spoke at the top of his voice.

"Don't believe her, boss! It is a trap. How is this possible?" Arian pleaded against her.

"Idiot! I am an officer. Why would I declare my change of mind before my team? Why would I express my whim to marry Devin there? You moron!

Have you ever used your mind?" She burst furiously.

The silence fell and the three looked at one another. It was not long before she picked up, "I knew you were going to get it, I could have sorcerized you and I could have foiled your aim." She breathed heavily as if tired of her justifications.

"We both make a perfect match. I know you are a handsome bachelor. We will rule the world forever." She proposed to Devin.

Devin burst into a laugh again, "How sweet of you! How romantic of you! Who will believe she is coming from her mother's funeral? Who will believe she is going to marry her mother's death angel?" He doffed his hat, pointing his index finger at her. He scrutinized her facial expressions and snapped, "You just want to get this emerald ring, you want to destroy it and expose us to the law. Right?"

"Absolutely yes! I'm asking for a trouble. I know you can read my mind. I've come here just for this emerald. I'll cadge it off you and perhaps destroy your Pyrus. I may kill you. My mother's blood is avenged. It is my design." Angela retorted sneeringly. She resumed, "You can even get this watch from me Devin. This magic watch has come into my life after my mother's life. I am a sorceress now."

"I have a condition that we get hitched on camera. You resign from your present job and live with me forever. What do you have to say to this?" Devin stared at her, demanding a pledge.

"I accept it on one condition that you expose him to public and media."

"What're you saying? You bitch!" Arian yelled, fuming over the situation.

"Do you accept it now?"

"I only want to rule this world and enslave the human race." He remarked.

"But who'll rule this world after you?" She made a strong point. She could see the varying expression on his face.

"I think it better to rub her out. She is going to split us apart. Boss!" Arian thundered with rage.

"Kill him, Devin, we'll live together. We don't need him." Angela pleaded, putting her head onto Devin's shoulder.

"I'll kill you!" Arian ran at her with a large tombstone.

No sooner had he thrown it at her head than he was ripped open by Pyrus. He fell lifeless to the ground.

"Devin, trust me! We are made for each other." She whispered to him, looking deep into his eyes.

"Confide your watch to me now." He demanded.

Angela removed her watch and began to hand him. But, he stopped her and said, "I believe you. You are right! Let bygones be bygones."

"I accept you. You are right about our wizard children."

"See my wrist watch has all magic gems. Your ring has the master magic emerald. We are to live to rule this world. I am sick of this drudgery."

Devin pulled the ring out of his finger and put it on hers. He was all too overwhelmed with this reformation to see or think of anything else. On the spur of the moment she drew the emerald ring and slung it to Faizan who was just there. He lit it up and crushed it underfoot as long as Devin was lost in her embrace.

Devin Yukol was pushed off and Angela was flung to the ground with force. The strong dark wind blew dust onto their faces and body. Some distance away her office driver was thrown to a gravestone. The wind turned into a ferocious dust storm which could blow over the treetops and loose heavy stones. Devin overbalanced and roared with all his wrath, "What've you done? Treason?"

Rising to her feet, Angela trudged through to him and plunged a sharp knife in his chest through his heart. He pulled it out and levitated himself high above her, recovering from the stab. He kicked her face two times from high above and knocked her over. She got back to her feet quickly and levitated level to him. Gathering all her strength and energies she dealt a series of hard blows to him, almost stunning him.

In the blink of an eye, she summoned her hallow to her service while Devin was still regaining his powers.

It did not occur to him that she had gained as many energies and powers as him. He roared again, "Arian was right. I killed him for you. You got revenge on me."

"Yes! Your Pyrus has perished and your accomplice is killed. It still doesn't make it even." Her voice reverberated through the whole town. She and Devin landed on the ground then her hermit appeared in front of them.

He summoned his powers to his help, chanting incantations until a horde of soaring demons swooped down to Angela and her hermit, but to little avail. Her hermit gyrated so fast that his arms pounded through them to dust. Although she was flown away by a few jinns that scratched and struck her, her bright glow loosened their grip on her and fought them off. She descended after her combat, shining the incandescence of her watch into Devin's eyes, which blinded him and confiscated all his evil powers.

He fell to the ground with a thud. She quickly grasped the knife in her right hand and tried to slit his throat. Out of the blue, the police and ambulance called in by Faizan arrived on the scene.

After a while, she opened her eyes in a hospital bed with her colleagues at her side.

Devin was also in the same hospital under medical observation. The investigation team was waiting for him to make a complete, speedy recovery which was needed for his admission and confession to the law. He was in the intensive care unit under senior doctors.

Angela was applauded by all her staff members, Devin Yukol made his confession statement to the police and he was jailed for life. Mr. Mathew Peter and Mrs. Monica were restored to their positions. Angela's case won international acclaims and she set an example for her department.